W9-BTK-456

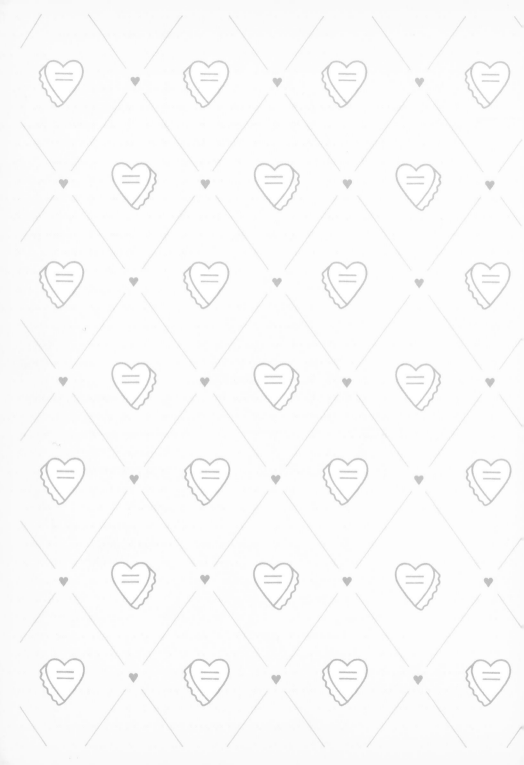

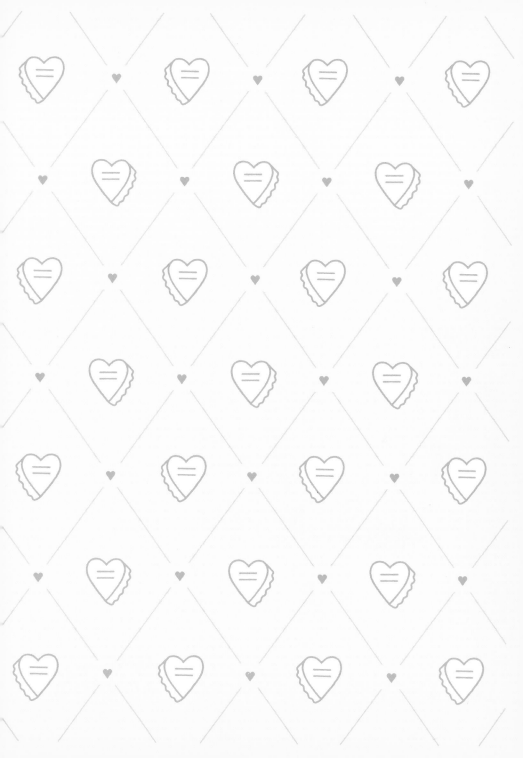

The QUEEN *of* HEARTS

Story and Pictures

by

Elizabeth Koda-Callan

WORKMAN PUBLISHING, NEW YORK

Copyright © 1995 by Elizabeth Koda-Callan

"Elizabeth Koda-Callan's Magic Charm Books" and the design/logo are
registered trademarks of Elizabeth Koda-Callan.

All rights reserved. No portion of this book may be reproduced—
mechanically, electronically, or by any other means, including
photocopying—without written permission of the publisher. Published
simultaneously in Canada by Thomas Allen & Son Limited.

Library of Congress Cataloging-in-Publication Data

Koda-Callan, Elizabeth.
The queen of hearts / by Elizabeth Koda-Callan.
p. cm.
Summary: A little girl promises that her mother will bake cookies for the
school party, but when her mother has to work late, the girl decides to do
it herself.
ISBN 0-7611-0167-5
[1. Baking—Fiction. 2. Cookies—Fiction. 3. Self-confidence—Fiction.]
I. Title. II. Series: Koda-Callan, Elizabeth, Elizabeth Koda-Callan's Magic
charm books.
PZ7.K8175Qu   1995
[E]—dc20   95-18351
                                                                CIP
                                                                 AC

Workman books are available at special discounts when purchased
in bulk for premiums and sales promotions, as well as for fundraising
or educational use. Special editions or book excerpts can
also be created to specification. For details, contact the
Special Sales Director at the address below.

Workman Publishing Company, Inc.
708 Broadway
New York, NY 10003
Printed in Hong Kong
First printing October 1995
10 9 8 7 6 5 4 3 2 1

For my mother and father,
Helen and Alexander Koda

Once there was a little girl who wanted to bake the most delicious cookies in the world. She dreamed of baking cookies fit for royalty.

It just so happened that her mother was a very good cookie maker, and the little girl loved to watch when she baked.

One Saturday, the little girl's mother said, "I feel like making chocolate cookies today. Would you like to help?"

"Oh, yes," answered the little girl excitedly. But that day she added too much flour and the cookies came out too dry.

The next time the little girl helped, she forgot to set the timer and the cookies burned on the bottom.

It seemed that *whenever* the little girl helped, the cookies never came out quite right. "Maybe I'm not cut out to be a baker," she sighed.

One day at school, the little girl's teacher announced that there was going to be a class party. "We'll need refreshments," she said. "Who would like to volunteer?"

The little girl's hand shot up. "I'll bring cookies," she said. "My mother makes the best cookies in the world."

The little girl couldn't wait to tell her mother all about the party. "I said I'd bring cookies, Mom. Can you make your tea hearts?"

"Of course, dear," replied her mother as she put her arm around the little girl. "We'll make them together."

Every day the little girl reminded her mother about the cookies. She didn't want *anything* to go wrong.

The day before the party, the little girl hurried home from school. She found her mother in the living room putting papers into her briefcase. "I can't wait to start the cookies," she said excitedly.

The little girl's mother sat down on the sofa. "I found out at work today that I have to leave on an important business trip. I'm afraid we're not going to be able to make the cookies for your party," her mother said gently.

"But, Mom, we *have* to," the little girl pleaded.

"I'm sorry, dear, but sometimes things come up that we can't help. We can always pick up some cookies at the store."

"Store-bought cookies?" cried the little girl. "I promised the class *homemade* cookies!"

The little girl was so upset that she could hardly bring herself to say goodbye.

After her mother left, the little girl rushed to her room. She stayed there for quite some time, thinking about what she could do. "If I don't want to buy the cookies, maybe I could make them myself," she thought.

Just then, there was a soft knock on the door. The little girl opened it. It was her father.

"I'll help you make the cookies," he offered.

"But, Dad, you never baked anything," said the little girl.

"I do make the best burgers in the house," he boasted. "How hard could it be?"

To the little girl, it seemed very hard indeed, but she certainly didn't want to go to school empty-handed. "Okay," she said, now sounding quite determined. "Let's give it a try."

Together, they hurried to the kitchen. The little girl put on an apron and rolled up her sleeves. Her father did the same.

"Mom and I were going to make tea hearts," she said as she took down the flour and sugar from the cupboard.

"What are tea hearts?" asked her father.

"They're the delicious shortbread cookies Mom makes," answered the little girl. "She rolls out the dough and cuts it into heart shapes. She calls them 'tea hearts' because she likes them with her tea. But I think they taste just as good with milk."

"Tea hearts it is," said the little girl's father.

The little girl and her father found the tea-heart recipe in her mother's favorite cook book. "First we need to pre-heat the oven," the little girl said as her father began to read the recipe aloud.

She then took the butter out of the refrigerator. "Mom says it's important to let the butter soften, so it's easier to blend," she told her father.

After carefully measuring all the ingredients, the little girl placed the softened butter in a big bowl and mixed in the sugar. She added the flour, one cup at a time. Then she and her father took turns stirring the mixture until they had a stiff dough.

"It looks like you learned a lot from watching Mom," he said as he helped her roll out the dough into a large rectangle.

"I guess I *have*," she said surprised at how much she remembered.

The little girl then found the old heart-shaped cookie cutter that her mother always used. It had scalloped edges and a little handle.

She cut heart-shaped cookies out of the dough and placed them on cookie sheets to bake until they turned golden brown.

Soon a delicious aroma filled the kitchen. And before long, the little girl and her father were admiring rows of freshly baked heart cookies cooling on wire racks.

"We did it!" said her father.

"Yes, but how do they taste?" asked the little girl. She reached for one of the cookies, broke it in half, and shared it with her father.

"Yummmmmm!" they said in unison after the first bite.

"These cookies are super," he said.

When the cookies were cool, the little girl dusted them with powdered sugar and placed them in a large cookie tin. Those that didn't fit, she put into the cookie jar on the counter.

The next morning, the little girl took the cookie tin to school. When it was time for the party, the whole class helped decorate and set the table with big plates of treats.

Everything was delicious, but the little girl couldn't help noticing that everyone kept coming back for more of her cookies.

While the little girl was getting something to drink, two classmates joined her at the table. Both of them were eating her tea hearts. "You were right," said one. "Your mother *does* make the best cookies."

"Actually," said the little girl, "my mother didn't make them. I did—with a little help from my dad."

"You made them?" said the other girl. "Wow! They're really great!"

The little girl had a wonderful time at the party, talking and laughing with her friends.

After school, the little girl was surprised to find her mother waiting for her.

"Mom," the little girl called out as she ran toward her. "You won't believe what happened!"

Her mother smiled. "Dad told me about the cookies you made. He said they were fit for a queen." She paused. "I wish I could have been there to help."

"That's okay, Mom," said the little girl. "Dad did just fine."

"Well, I'd love to hear all about it and about your party, too," her mother said as they walked together.

When they reached home, the little girl ran to open the cookie jar and proudly presented the tea hearts to her mother. "I saved some for you, Mom," she said.

"Ummm, delicious!" her mother said after taking a bite. "This calls for a celebration. But first, I have something for you."

The little girl's mother pulled a small pink flannel drawstring pouch from her briefcase and handed it to the little girl. Inside was a silver heart-shaped charm on a glittery silver chain. It was a tiny version of the cookie cutter that the little girl had used for the tea hearts. "Ohh!" the little girl said in astonishment.

"This is a special charm for a budding baker," said her mother. "I'm very proud of you for making the cookies yourself."

The little girl beamed and gave her mother a hug. Her mother helped her put on the beautiful new necklace.

Now I'll make the tea and you pour the milk. And we'll have a tea-heart party of our own," said her mother. The little girl thought that was a splendid idea.

"To the Queen of Hearts," exclaimed her mother, lifting her cup. The little girl told her mother all about the school party as they finished the tea-heart cookies. They had a royal good time.

That day, the little girl *did* feel like the Queen of Hearts.

About the Author

Elizabeth Koda-Callan is a designer, illustrator, and best-selling children's book author who lives in New York City. Her favorite cookies to make as a child were oatmeal crisps.

She is the creator of the Magic Charm book series, which includes THE MAGIC LOCKET, THE SILVER SLIPPERS, THE GOOD LUCK PONY, THE TINY ANGEL, THE SHINY SKATES, THE CAT NEXT DOOR, and THE TWO BEST FRIENDS.

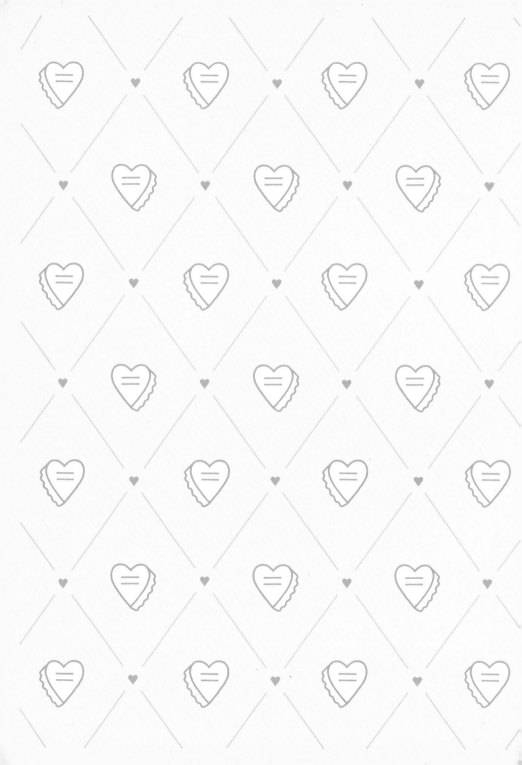